ARTEO

ARTEO

Kaitlyn and Sandy Brannin

To: Will

Dream Big !!!

Love, Kaitlyn Brannin

Sandy Brannin

VANTAGE PRESS
New York

Illustrated by Tanya Stewart

FIRST EDITION

Published by Vantage Press, Inc.
419 Park Ave. South, New York, NY 10016

Manufactured in the United States of America
ISBN: 978-0-533-16229-1

Library of Congress Catalog Card No: 2009903565

0 9 8 7 6 5 4 3

Manufactured by BookMasters
Ashland, OH (USA)
M7131   Mar. 2010

ARTEO

1

Katie and Mike were in their backyard playing on the swing set. It was a beautiful summer day. There was a warm, gentle breeze, the type that feels so good it makes your skin tingle and makes you feel happy. The sky was blue and the trees were swaying gently in the breeze. You could almost smell the warmth in the air. A dog was barking just down the street as some kids rode their bikes outside.

Katie and Mike were so happy and excited. School had just let out. Katie had just completed the second grade and her little brother, Mike, kindergarten. Katie was swinging on the swing with her dark brown hair falling in her face with each kick to go higher. Her hazel eyes sparkled in the sun. She was daydreaming and thinking about spending her summer trying to start a dog-sitting business. Katie wants to be a veterinarian when she grows up.

Mike was on the swing to Katie's left. He is good at swinging high but not as good as he is at baseball. As he was swinging he started laughing out loud.

"What is so funny?" asked Katie.

Mike was remembering the time he hit a baseball so hard one day it went up in the air and he never saw

it come down. He started to get a crooked smile on his face.

Katie and Mike have been spending most of the spring outside after school playing games. They played tag, wrestled and jumped on the trampoline a lot. Their favorite thing to do is to pretend they are having wild and fun adventures together.

"So Mike, what do you want to do this summer?" asked Katie.

"I don't know, what do you want to do?" replied Mike.

"Wouldn't it be fun if we could have an adventure together?" said Katie.

Mike agreed. They kept playing on the swing set and were swinging higher and higher.

"You want to jump off and see who makes it the farthest?" asked Mike.

"Ok," replied Katie, "on the count of three. One, two, three!" and they jumped off the swings together, but they did not land.

They were flying! UP, UP, UP they went above the treetops. The wind was blowing in their hair. They looked at each other in surprise.

"What's happening?" asked Mike.

"I don't know," said Katie.

They were scared and their eyes were as big as golfballs. The kids saw a flock of birds and flew right past them. Katie and Mike were still going up, but they were starting to have a lot of fun now. Their hands were clenched together as tight as they could hold. Katie's fingers were starting to turn white where Mike was squeezing so hard.

They looked at each other and smiled. "This is fun!" Mike yelled.

Katie and Mike started going faster now, and the wind was getting warmer. The sky started to sparkle and the clouds seemed to be changing shapes. "That cloud looks like a turtle, and that one a fish, and over there a dog!" yelled Katie.

Mike agreed. The clouds seemed to be changing into animal shapes. The sky was blue but had tints of pink, yellow, and white. It looked like there were sparkles everywhere. The sparkles were shaped like snowflakes, each one was different and they looked like pieces of shiny crystal glass.

Katie and Mike started to fly slower now and were getting lower in the sky. They were still holding hands as tight as they could. The siblings were going down. As Katie and Mike got lower in the sky, they could see trees more green and more beautiful than they had ever seen before. The trees were the color of a Christmas tree on Christmas Day. They were so full of leaves you could not see through them. Katie and Mike landed on their feet in the thick green grass right next to a stream. The grass came up just above Katie and Mike's ankles and tickled their legs as the wind blew gently.

The stream was the color of a bluebird and had small ripples throughout that glistened in the sunlight.

The far side of the bank was covered in the same thick green grass and had a rock that was gray and the size of a small car. It was so peaceful and quiet.

2

Katie and Mike heard birds singing. The birds' song sounded like a lullaby. Katie said, "Look over there!" Mike turned his head and saw a waterfall—but it was like no waterfall he had seen before. It was taller than any building he had ever seen and it looked like a rainbow. The water flowing down was purple, pink, red, yellow and orange. When the water hit the stream, it became a beautiful deep blue. "It's the most beautiful thing I have ever seen," said Katie.

Mike bumped his elbow against Katie's arm and said, "Shhh! Do you hear that!"

"Hear what?" asked Katie.

"That sound," said Mike.

Katie listened very carefully. "What is it?" she asked.

"I don't know," said Mike. "It sounds like something really big is walking toward us."

They both cowered as they heard the tree branches moving as something approached. "I'm scared," said Mike.

Katie and Mike held hands and turned around very slowly. Standing in front of them was the most amazing thing they had ever seen. It was a unicorn. It was big and beautiful with white fur and white feathers on its

7

wings. In the center of his head was a golden horn that shone in the sunlight. The unicorn had a black nose and gentle black eyes. He had a very muscular body and stood up tall. He was at least twice as tall as Katie.

"Hello," said the unicorn. "I am Solomon."

"Katie, that unicorn is talking to us," said Mike. "Animals are not supposed to talk."

"Why aren't we?" said Solomon.

"They don't talk at home," said Mike.

"Be quiet," said Katie. "Where are we?" she asked Solomon.

"This is Arteo," said Solomon, "my home. What kind of animal are you? I have never seen a creature here before like you."

"I am not an animal!" said Mike. "I am a boy!"

"What is a boy?" asked Solomon.

Katie looked at Mike and said, "I think that we are in a different land."

"What land is it that you come from?" asked Solomon.

"We are from West Virginia," said Katie.

"What are your names?" asked Solomon.

"I am Katie, and this is my brother, Mike. We were at home swinging on our swing set, and now we are here. We really don't even know where *here* is," said Katie.

"Let me take you to my home and give you food and water. You will meet my family, and we will try to help you," said Solomon.

3

Katie and Mike talked it over and decided that they should go with the unicorn. They followed Solomon through the woods. All the trees were a deep emerald green, and the limbs were swaying in the gentle breeze almost like the arms of a ballerina. The trees looked just like the oak trees back home but seemed more alive, like they were dancing. The birds were singing, but now Katie and Mike realized that they were singing in words they could understand. They saw squirrels, rabbits, deer, and a baby bear on their way to Solomon's house. The baby bear waved at them and said, "Hello." Katie said "Hi" back to the bear, but Mike just kept walking with his mouth wide open. He couldn't believe what was happening.

Solomon, Katie, and Mike came up to a small house in the woods. The house sat in a small clearing and was shaded from the bright sun above. It was shaped like a small barn. The sides were made of brown wood and the roof was covered in tree leaves and twigs. The door was very large and in the shape of a vertical rectangle. It was white and had a gray horseshoe on the front of it that was hanging upside down. There were two windows on the front of the house on either side of the door, no shutters. The windows were larger than the

ones at Katie and Mike's house, but they could not see in them. Everything about the house was very peaceful and welcoming. There were small patches of clover on the ground in front of the house. Katie loved it.

"Welcome to my home," said Solomon.

Katie and Mike followed him into his house. The floor of the house was dirt that was packed down. There was a room to the right that Katie and Mike would have called a family room at home. It had some clover plants and a bowl of oats on the table in the center of the room. To the left was the kitchen, and standing there was a beautiful purple unicorn. Her horn was golden, like Solomon's, and her wings were light pink. She looked as soft as a baby kitten. She was baking cookies that were made out of corn and nuts while humming a tune.

"This is my wife Sadie," said Solomon. "Sadie, I found this boy and girl in the woods next to the stream. They are from a land called West Virginia. I thought maybe we could try and help them."

Sadie turned around with a startled look on her face. "Solomon, what are you doing bringing these strange animals into our house! You know that it is not safe here!" Sadie exclaimed. Solomon walked over to Sadie, and they started talking privately in the kitchen.

Katie started to walk around a little and saw some photos on the wall. There was a picture of Solomon, Sadie and two smaller unicorns. "Are these your children?" she asked.

Sadie dropped her head down and started to cry.

Solomon hung his head as well and said, "Yes, they were taken from us two days ago by the Hawk and his helpers. Sit down kids, and let me explain it to you. You may be in danger here."

Katie and Mike sat down on the ground and began to listen to Solomon.

"The Hawk lives deep in these woods. For many years he lived in his nest home at the top of the tallest mountain. He never talked to anyone nor came down from his home unless he needed food or water. A few months ago one of the squirrels said that the Hawk came down and carried off their oldest son and they haven't seen their son since. There have been many reports since then of kids being taken away by the Hawk or his helpers. We do not know why. Some say that he is keeping them in his nest home and making them slaves. We will let you stay here for the night, but you must return home as soon as you can," Solomon said.

Sadie led Katie and Mike to one of the bedrooms after dinner. It was the kids' room. There were two beds on the ground made of hay. Sadie dropped a blanket over each bed. Katie took one bed and Mike the other.

"I can't sleep," said Mike.

"Me either," said Katie. "I feel so bad for Solomon and Sadie. They are so nice and so sad. I don't understand why the Hawk would do something so terrible. We have to do something to help them."

"What can we do?" asked Mike.

"I don't know but we must find a way to help," Katie said with determined eyes.

4

It was morning. Katie and Mike were just waking up as the sun came in through the bedroom window.

"Suddenly Mike sat up in bed and said, "Katie, wake up quick! I had a crazy dream last night! We were on the swings and then started flying and ended up in another land."

Katie rubbed her eyes and said, "Funny I had a dream like that too." They both stood up and looked out the window and realized that it was not just a dream.

Katie and Mike walked into the kitchen. Sadie and Solomon were there. There was also a deer in their kitchen. He was very tall and looked very strong. He had at least twelve antlers on his head. His eyes were as black as coal and very sad. Katie and Mike could hear them talking.

"My son was taken last night," said the deer. "He just went out of the den to get a drink and was carried off by several flying animals. They were too quick and I could not get to my son fast enough to stop them. They flew to the west."

His head hung low as he told his story. Then he saw Mike and Katie and turned around quickly.

"Who are you?" he asked with a stern tone.

Solomon said, "These are two kids from West

Virginia I found in the woods by the stream last night. They are not from here and needed somewhere to stay for the night, since it is not safe in the woods."

The deer looked at Solomon for a minute, then huffed and said, "I am Broto."

"I am Katie, and this is my brother Mike," Katie said. "I am very sorry that your son was taken. Is there anything that we can do to help?"

"I don't see how," said Broto sadly.

"We must find a way to get you kids home before the Hawk finds you," said Sadie.

"How are you going to do that?" asked Mike.

"I don't know," said Solomon. He thought for a minute, then said, "Maybe we can take the kids to the wise owl, Valsar. He may have an idea of how to get them back home."

5

Katie and Mike said good-bye to Sadie after a breakfast of oats and fruit and followed Solomon and Broto through the woods. They were making their way to Valsar's tree. All the animals watched with curious faces as Katie and Mike walked by. There were many animals out playing with their kids in the woods.

"Aren't they afraid of the Hawk?" asked Katie.

"The Hawk only comes out when the sun starts to go down," replied Solomon. "We are safe now."

They arrived at Valsar's home. Valsar lived in a very old oak tree in the forest. The opening to his home was far off the ground, and you could see it through the weakened tree limbs. The group stood at the base of the tree for about two minutes. Then suddenly an owl swooped down and landed on the tree branch above them. He was brown, with white tips on the end of his wings and black tips on the end of his tail. He watched like he was waiting for something.

Solomon spoke first and explained to Valsar how Katie and Mike had arrived in Arteo. Valsar listened long and hard to Solomon's words. After Solomon finished, Valsar said that he would come up with a plan to get the children home. While the animals were talking, Katie and Mike were whispering back and forth.

"Is there something you want to say, kids?" asked Valsar.

"We want to try and help Solomon and Broto find their kids before we go home," said Katie. Mike agreed, but he was a little scared and trying very hard not to show it.

Valsar sat quietly for several minutes. "Maybe there is a way you can help" he said.

The Hawk had never seen humans before, and Valsar thought that maybe Katie and Mike could serve as a distraction. While the Hawk and his guards were watching Katie and Mike, Solomon, Broto, and some of the other parents would try to rescue the kids the Hawk had taken.

The five of them sat by the stream all day and came up with a plan. Quickly the news spread, from the birds to the squirrels to the deer and rabbits and all the animals in the woods. They had a rescue plan.

Solomon and Broto led Katie and Mike back to Solomon's house. Sadie was glad to see the kids this time. "Welcome back," she said. She turned to Solomon, "Did you have any luck finding a way to get Katie and Mike home?"

"I think so," replied Solomon, "but they have offered to try and help us get our children back first."

Sadie looked at Katie and Mike with tears of joy in her eyes. "Are you sure?" she said.

"Positive," said Katie.

"Thank you so much. You don't know what this means to us." Sadie walked up to Katie and Mike and put her long neck up to theirs to hug them. "Let me take you to your room for the night so you may rest," she said.

6

The next day, Katie and Mike were led deep into the woods by Valsar to where the Hawk's nest was. Mike looked up at the mountain. It was very high and it had dark grey clouds looming over the peak. There were no green trees on the mountain like the rest of Arteo, only rocks and dead trees on the mountainside. Mike kept looking and saw the Hawk's nest. It was black and built with dead trees and branches. It was crooked and not built well. It looked like a haunted house. Mike shuddered as a chill went down his spine.

"I don't think this is a good idea anymore," said Mike. "What if the Hawk takes us?"

"Remember what Solomon said—the Hawk only takes the kids at night. It is the middle of the day," Katie replied.

Mike was still scared, but he continued with the plan. They were to play games in the meadow below the Hawk's nest. The children would get the attention of the Hawk's guards and serve as a distraction.

Katie and Mike started to play. "Not It, said Mike. Katie was It and chased Mike. They were playing tag. Soon a bunch of big birds started to watch them play. The birds were dark brown and had a wide wingspan. They had cold, dark eyes and sharp claws. The birds sat

on the branches of the trees above and watched Katie and Mike play and laugh. The birds thought this was very funny, since they had never seen kids before. Next, Katie and Mike started wrestling and tickling each other. They were laughing as hard as they could. More birds were coming to watch, and it sounded like the birds were laughing too.

As Katie and Mike played and distracted the Hawk's guards, Solomon, Broto, and the other animals started to sneak into the Hawk's nest. Katie and Mike stuck to their plan and kept on entertaining the birds.

Suddenly there was a very loud noise coming from the nest. It sounded like the cracking and breaking of trees. Large birds started flying everywhere and small animals came running out of the nest as fast as they could. Katie and Mike heard so many high-pitched squealing noises that their ears started to ring.

Solomon swooped down from the sky. "Quick—hop on!" he yelled. Katie and Mike didn't hesitate and hopped on Solomon's broad back as he ran across the meadow and started to fly away. There were two smaller unicorns following right behind Solomon.

"Look, down there!" yelled Katie. They saw Broto with his son running back into the woods. His son was much smaller than Broto and had only three antlers on his head. All the other kid animals were running home with their parents as well.

"Come back, come back!" someone behind them was yelling in a very angry voice. It was the Hawk and he was following everyone out of the nest. Some bears were waiting for him and grabbed the Hawk as he flew out of the nest.

"Ha, ha" said Mike. He turned toward Solomon and said, "I guess he won't be bothering you again," with a grin from ear to ear.

7

Solomon landed on the green grass beside the stream where Katie and Mike had arrived just two days ago. The two smaller unicorns were his kids, Max and Claire. Max was white and brown and Claire was purple with pink wings. They were standing next to Solomon, nuzzling each other. Sadie had just arrived and joined her family in their celebration.

"They are so beautiful," said Katie. "Look how happy they are together," she said to Mike.

Mike started to get tears in his eyes.

"What's wrong?" said Katie.

"Nothing," sniffed Mike. "It just makes me miss Mom and Dad."

"Me too," said Katie.

Valsar swooped down. "I think that it is about time we got you kids home. We all owe you our thanks. None of us would have our families back together if it wasn't for your help."

Broto ran out of the woods with his son right behind him. Mike's eyes got as big as the moon when Broto leaned forward to give him a big hug.

Katie reached out her arms and hugged Broto. "Thank you," he said.

"You are welcome," she said to him and all her new friends.

"I am ready to go home now," said Mike. "Me too," said Katie, "but I will miss you all very much." She got tears in her eyes as she thought about leaving Arteo forever. "Is there a way we can ever come back and visit?"

"That would be a lot of fun," said Mike, "as long as the Hawk is not around."

"I don't think you will have to worry about that—the bears will keep a good eye on him," said Solomon.

"How are we going to get home?" asked Katie.

Valsar flew over and sat on Solomon's back and started to whisper in his ear. "It is time to say good-bye now," said Valsar.

Katie and Mike walked around and gave each of their new friends a big hug. "I hope I can come back and play with all your kids one day," Mike said to Solomon and Broto.

Valsar smiled a big smile. "Maybe one day, when the moon is full and the wind is blowing just right, you will find your way here again. Just never forget how all this started," he said. Then he flew off.

8

"Hop on, kids. Time to go," said Solomon.

Katie and Mike jumped on his back and they started to fly. As they were flying Mike said, "Katie, look over there!" All the animals were standing in the clearing by the stream now. They were waving and saying good-bye. Katie and Mike waved back with smiles on their faces.

"Where are you taking us, Solomon?" asked Katie.

"You will see," he said. "Just do as I say and you will get home safely."

Solomon flew closer and closer to the waterfall. "What are you doing?" yelled Mike.

"Hold hands!" yelled Solomon. "Now count to three and jump."

"You're crazy!" said Katie.

"Trust me," said Solomon. "I wouldn't hurt you. You saved my kids."

Katie and Mike grabbed each other's hands as tight as they could and looked into each other's eyes. Together they counted, "One, two, three," and then they jumped off of Solomon and into the waterfall. Then Katie and Mike started to see sparkles in the sky and funny clouds again, just like they did when they were flying to Arteo. The air was getting warmer and the hairs on Katie and Mike's

arms were sticking up. Suddenly they started falling. "*Ahhhhhh!*" They both yelled together.

Katie and Mike hit the ground and started rolling. "Are you okay?" asked Katie.

"Yeah, I'm fine," said Mike. "Are you okay?"

"Yes," said Katie.

"Look!" yelled Mike as he pointed his finger behind them.

They were back in their yard. The swings were still swinging as if they had just jumped off them. It was like Katie and Mike had never been gone. They turned toward each other and hugged tightly.

"I guess that counts as a summer adventure," said Katie. They both stood up and started walking toward the back of their house.

"I want to go back tomorrow," said Mike.

"Me too," said Katie.

They smiled and held hands as they walked through the back door.